GLORY, PRESENCE, AND THE REIGN OF GOD

IN JOHN'S GOSPEL

(EXPLORATIONS IN CARIBBEAN EMANCIPATORY THEOLOGY)

ABOUT THE COVER

The image on the cover depicts a hummingbird in its glory. One of the possible translations for the aboriginal name of the island of Trinidad Iere has been "Land of the Hummingbird", because of the place given to this species as a manifestation of the presence of God amongst his people. The Celts have their Wild Goose and the Jews the dove, as seen in the baptism of our Lord in John 1: 32 and as the Baptiser bore witness that the Holy Spirit came upon Jesus in this form and rested on him. The hummingbird has always been sacred to these parts much like the dove is related to the Holy Spirit in the Bible.

In Trinidad and Tobago, there is the legend of how the Pitch Lake at La Brea came to be. It is the story of a village of Chaima Indians [for whom Carapichaima is named], who against the demands of the gods but in obedience to their cacique's wishes, decimated a flock of hummingbirds and took the plumes to decorate the king's robes. In ire, they were punished when their village sank beneath the earth and was covered by thick asphalt never to rise again. The tale has been preserved for all time by the Rev'd. William Henry Brett, Anglican missionary to the Native Guiana Indians in the latter half of the 19th century, in his poem, "Warau Ideas Concerning Departed Souls.'

"When Waraus were, as we have shown,
Oppressed by stronger foes,
The fears which they through life had known
Beset them at its close.
Each charged his children when he died
To place his weapons at his side.

Lay bow and arrows in my grave,
That I may keep at bay
The souls of foemen fierce and brave,
And all who bar my way.
My soul, thus armed, none dare withstand,
To keep it from the spirit land!
How different was the legend told
On Trinidad's fair isle;
Where Waraus gathered fruits of old
And rested there awhile;
Where souls of good men they could find
In glittering humming birds enshrined!

Those birds, like flashing jewels seen,
Bedecked each lovely bower.
As ruby, topaz, emerald green,
They kissed each fragrant flower,
And saw fair hills and forests rise
Around their blissful paradise.

But Chaymas dared those birds molest,
Then—sank beneath the ground!
And now, where happy souls had rest,
The lake of pitch is found.
Wild Warau myth of ages past—
To English readers told at last" (1)

Indeed, this sentiment forms the basis for the thought behind the composing of a number of Latin American Psalms rooted deep within the liberation and Caribbean emancipatory theological expression. The particular psalm entitled, "A Psalm of Indigenous Peoples" bears this thought out. Originally composed in Brazilian Portuguese, it is here reproduced by the writer in English.

"Hear, O Lord of all the peoples,
Maira in the origin of all things

Our first father Nhamandu.
Oh hear our voice that comes from the depths of our bewilderment,
From the multitude of our dead,
From our countless sorrows.
Preserve life for us, from the conspiracy of evildoers
And from the iniquitous schemes of the powerful.
They require of us our land,
They flood our jungles,
They buy and sell our lives and our cultures,
They despise our millennial wisdom.
They devise iniquity upon iniquity,
And their heart is a bottomless pit.
Yet do we believe in you,
We celebrate your name,
We rejoice in your mystery,
We sing of your glory,
In that you love us and make us glad.
Yes, O Mystery of Life,
You shoot an arrow against them
And at once they are wounded.
They will stumble and their own tongue will turn against them.
Will they ever learn to respect your name
And welcome other peoples as kinsfolk?
This is what we hope for, in faith.for ever, preferred
Help them to be different.
Only then will we be joyful and extend our hands, without fear,
As brothers and sisters.
You who created the earth beautiful,
The jungles, the rivers, the fish and all animals,
May you be blessed for ever. Amen." (2).

NOTES:
1. William Henry Brett, Legends and Myths of the Aboriginal Indians of British Guiana

[London, 1880] {Reduced to HTML by Christopher M. Weimer, March 2003}, http://www.sacred-texts.com/nam/sa/lmbg/index.htm

2. Salmos Latino Americanos {Latin American Psalm), Paulinas S.P. Brasil, published in Seeing the Situation, Listening to Hope, Liturgical Resources for Worship at the 3rd Encounter of Bishops and Pastors from Latin America and the Caribbean, Rio de Janeiro 1993, Psalm of Indigenous Peoples, pg. 50.

INTRODUCTION

In evangelical circles, the Gospel of John is generally commended as the book to read to gain an introduction to the Christian faith. It is of an intensely personal and spiritual nature, yet it is written in a highly philosophical Greek argumentative style, from the very resonance of its opening appeal to reason and logic in the prologue.

This work seeks to focus on the 'signs of glory' in John; several miraculous experiences that are not recorded in either Matthew, Mark, or Luke, but which are unique to John. It has come out of numerous years of lecturing on and study in the Person and Work of Jesus Christ, at the level of the Codrington College Diploma in Theological Studies, Trinidad and Tobago Campus, and administered through the Sehon Goodridge Theological Society, of which the writer is a founder and governing member. It is also tinged, inevitably, with the brush of a Caribbean contextual theology, as present-day theologians come once again to grapple with the realities of selfhood and identity, and identification with the local landscape on which our forebears were rerooted from ancestral lands, in a new and generally hostile milieu, out of which have further come new ways of seeing and being.

The evangelist, or gospel writer, John, had to choose from a wide array of accounts and experiences of his own and also those circulating within the nascent Christian community, of things Jesus said and did, Jn 20: 30, 21: 25. The description of these acts by John is in the use of the word 'sign' or *semeion* in the Greek. For the Synoptics, these are stupendous miracles, acts of power and glory, *dunameis*, mighty works of The One who operates in the power and authority of YHWH. For John, these are signs pointing to something, signs of glory. Seven miracles of Jesus are usually said to be recorded: The changing of water into wine, the healing of the Official's son, the healing of the paralytic by the Pool of Bethesda (more specifically called a 'work' not a 'sign' per se), the feeding of the five thousand, the walking on water (although this is technically never called a 'sign' in John nor does it specifically function as one), the healing of the man born blind, and the raising of Lazarus.

But to what does glory refer? For this, we have to turn to the Prologue where we find our pivotal verse 1: 14 viz. "And the Word became flesh and lived among us, and we have seen his glory, the glory as of a father's only son, full of grace and truth." The word 'glory' usually points to something bright and dazzling as is referenced by the Hebrew word, *shekinah*. However, another Hebrew word seems more poignant here, *chabod*, which refers to the real presence of God as manifested in the Old Testament by the Ark of the Covenant (ref. 1 Sam. 4: 21-22). John also uses 'glory' in reference to Jesus' passion and death as per Jn. 12, whereas the Synoptic writers generally reference 'glory' as relating to power and authority through miracles and the second appearing in judgement (ref. Matt. 25: 31). But for our purposes in regard to Jn. 1: 14, we see glory as the manifest presence of God on earth in the incarnation of his child, Jesus. Glory is therefore incarnational, The Word became Flesh, and we have seen his Glory. John is declaring that the eternal reality of God was enfleshed in time and space in an historical human person, of real flesh and blood, who lived, died, and lived again. The major theme of these signs in John, therefore, is the manifestation of the presence of God on earth in the person and work of Jesus, and through this manifest presence, the reign of God is inaugurated on the earth. God has come to take personal and intimate possession of his special creation. This is a moral obligation on God's part since human sinfulness and rebellion to become like God(s) have created such a gulf between full and open communion (Gen. 2-3). This is not so much a matter of a trespassing of presence as a trespassing of nature and personhood on the part of humankind, but which incidentally is bridged not by humankind's becoming God but by God becoming Man in the incarnation of Jesus Christ his Son.

Perhaps the most familiar figure of Trinidad and Tobago folklore is that of the ancient Papa Bois, Father of the Forest. He is as ancient as the forests, rivers, and hills and he dwells in and among them. He is old and very hairy, but muscular and powerful. His feet are cloven hooves, and his beard is long and matted with leaves woven throughout his hairy frame. His face is grotesque, and he has a horn on either side of his brow. And like the Christian St. Giles, he has a deer for his constant companion, because he can be kind and gentle towards those who respect the creation but judgemental against those who take it for granted. He resembles the Old Testament image of God, the All-Terrible who can create as well as destroy; kind, merciful and gracious as well as displaying righteous indignation at humanity's rebelliousness. This God is sovereign in all his ways so that what passes as evil in the human realm, is commended as God's almightiness, who works in all and through all to bring his good will and pleasure to pass.

Papa Bois is the guardian of the forest and its dwellers. No act escapes his knowledge, being pervasive as the wind. Found at once in Aripo, El Tucuche, Tamana, and Moruga, he is one of the watchers and holy ones (elohim), spoken of in Daniel 4:16, who give account to God of humankind's deeds and execute God's judgement upon them. He tolerates no wanton killing of animals or abuse of its vegetation or produce, yet recognises that humans have a need of the land's sustenance. He is the custodian of the wild places, like the cherub that guards the Garden of Eden from humankind's ultimate craving for total world domination and devastation. He is as elusive yet as priestly as Melchizedek, the king and priest of Salem (Jerusalem) who dwells on Mt. Zion and who offers the fruit of the earth for human refreshment (Gen. 14:18). Like the God of Isaiah's holy mountain, he ensures that, "They shall not hurt or destroy in all my holy mountain..." (Isa. 11: 8).

This Father of the Forest demands due and proper homage and respect. If one ever chances to see him, obeisance is due in the form of a greeting of the day and traditionally in French, "Bon jour, vieux Papa!" But he is hardly seen since he is at many times at one with the creation so that his very being is in communion with the trees and the animals. He looks human yet he is distinct from the race, a transcendent yet wholly other being. As such, he represents not only one part of the earthly 'oikoumene', but the sum total of it, and evinces the interconnectedness of every facet of the universe. If ever he is seen, one must never look at his feet. His cloven hooves are taboo because they would reveal yet another domain for human curiosity, domination by knowledge, and eventual subjugation and possible extinction. As a matter of fact, it is taboo to look at the feet of any spirit except perhaps La Diablesse, who uses her feet to ensnare the unsuspecting lecher. It would be like seeing the glorious face of God in this mortal dress and living to tell the tale of one whom not even God's holiness was able to conquer and so become stronger than God himself (Ex. 33: 18-23), or of wrestling with God like Jacob (Gen. 32), and not only prevailing but overpowering and getting to know his name is able to invoke it at any time for any cause thus making God subject to the will of a mortal. This is quite different from God's revelation of the 'sacred name' to Moses in Exodus 3, which is more the revelation of the highest quality of his nature as the 'Self-Existent One' rather than a name that can be invoked like some magical charm. Christianity has tended to veer close to the edge with the use of the name of Jesus, by virtue of his resurrection, the name that is above every other name (Phil 2: 5-11), to which every other must bow in dominical subjection. Jesus, in casting out the demons from the Gardarene demoniac, asks the spirit[s] first its name so as to subject it to himself (Lk. 8: 26-39). When Christians use the name of Jesus it is not to make him bow to the demands of the one who invokes it, but rather the continuing announcement of his presence in the world through his body the Church and the assertion of his dominion, not humankind's or the church's over the created order.

According to A. M. Hunter (1), for John these signs demonstrate the kingdom or reign of God in action, whereas in the Synoptics the miracles of Jesus proclaim that the kingdom is drawing near. In other words, the reign of God is made present in the Christ Event, it is here and now, right before our very eyes. There is no need to proclaim its coming; it has already come and is showing itself in the works Jesus performs. As such, the miracles in John are signs that we are already in the age of the reign of God. It is not a future event. It is a realised eschatology. Eternal life is an experience to be grasped and lived here and now, not to be expected only after this life. For John, this life of the reign of God is a very present reality.

This overarching theme, found in Jn. 1: 14, will be examined through five of the seven signs in John, along with various sub-themes also mined from the Prologue, namely: the changing of water into wine, the healing of the paralytic, the feeding of the five thousand, the healing of the man born blind, and the raising of Lazarus. The Prologue is not merely the opening words of a piece of work; it operates here as the 'fount of all honour', as it were, from which every theme and issue in the gospel flows. It tells us what will be discussed. In the classic Aristotelian argumentative style it lays the foundation of the evangelist's thesis pivoted on that verse 14, and throughout the gospel and more particularly as concerns us here, in these five signs, the thesis and one or more of its sub-themes are presented and discussed, the antithesis argued, in which problems that arise from the thesis are examined; the critical word on which the thesis is founded. Through this, we arrive at a synthesis or conclusion proving and reinforcing the original thesis.

NOTE:
1. A. M. Hunter, According to John, SCM Press, London 1968, pg. 69, The Miracles in St. John

THE FIRST SIGN

CHANGING WATER INTO WINE – JOHN 2: 1-11
Jesus did this, the first of his signs, in Cana of Galilee, and revealed his glory; and his disciples believed in him.
Jn. 2: 11

This sign has generally been interpreted as symbolising the fulfilment of the Old Testament in the coming of Jesus. The first wine which was good and tasty enough had run its course and is replaced by the best wine one could give. It is a reversal of the norm where the best would be given and then when tongues have become too satiated and numb to savour anything substantial, an inferior product would then be offered to satisfy just the basic of cravings.

But we are to hinge our sign on the pivot of Jn 1: 14, and immediately we encounter our problem. In response to the plea of his mother, Jesus remarks that his hour had not yet come; a statement that resonates with the one made in Jn. 12: 23 when he states then that the hour had indeed come for him to be glorified. Jesus has in mind here, in Cana of Galilee, the hour of his ultimate glorification. Thus, for him, it was not time for that understanding and experience of glory to be manifested.

The problem is rectified if we recognise that John bears no distinct record of an institution of the Eucharist, although other scenes from the Last Supper are displayed. He does, however, give a hint of this sacramental institution in chapter 6 at the feeding of the five thousand where Jesus talks of himself as the Bread of Life and his flesh and blood as very meat and drink to be eaten and drunk. Here at the wedding feast, the new and best wine, the other major element of the Eucharist, is given; a motif that points to the wine of the kingdom, at the marriage feast of the Lamb. It is the bridegroom who is supposed to supply the drink at the feast and in this case, is unable to do so. Jesus steps in as the ultimate bridegroom who endows his bride, the Church, through the shedding of his blood symbolised in the wine of eternal or aeonian life; *aionios* being the Greek word meaning eternal. So that the wine, pointing to his blood further gives way to the shedding of his blood at his ultimate glory and glorification when his 'hour would have come'. Hence wine becomes a potent sign of the life of the age to come, aeonian life/eternal life/resurrection life. Wine, aged properly, never goes bad, it only gets better and maturer. Grape juice, on the other hand, will go bad on its own without refrigeration, but still eventually will go bad. However, the life of the age to come can never regress into its former state of corruption and decomposition but is a process of ever being "changed from glory into glory," (2 Cor. 3: 18). As such, wine is most appropriate for use at celebrations of the Eucharist because it portends the resurrection life of the age to come, and not grape juice, which speaks only to this life with all its failings and futility. It makes us question how high and how far churches set their goals, whether for this life only or for the one to come (1 Cor. 15: 19).

The thesis is further reinforced by seeing Jesus' glory as Lord of nature, the one coming to take possession of all he has made, as in Jn 1: 3 the sub-theme states, "All things came into being through him, and without him not one thing came into being." As Lord of nature, he not only has control over all he has made but takes ownership as the Greek word, *Kyrios,* and the Latin, *Dominus,* imply. It is further seen in the fact that Jesus performs no action or ritual (or 'semi-demi', as we say locally) to transform the nature of the water; quite unlike the "pastor" who secretly stuffed a red drink powder under his fingernails, had a large bucket of water brought to him, and then proceeded to pass his hand in the water at which point the powder dissolved and changed the water's colour, and the "pastor" cried out that he had performed a miracle similar to what Jesus was doing here! The hour of his glory as per Jn. 12 is again referenced in this motif when he declares that is the hour of the world's judgement when the pretended owner, the prince of this world would be cast out, and he takes full possession as Cosmic Overlord.

In these two motifs, the reign or kingdom of God is no longer a distant, far-off goal. It has come near, indeed it has broken into the world with the Word becoming human like us, moving into our neighbourhood and dwelling among us as one of us. The destination of all Jesus' preaching and teaching was and is the reign of God, the new age of a higher quality of life, aeonian life that begins here and now and finds consummation and bliss in the life of the world to come. For John, this eternal life does not begin at death but rather in the here and now where new wine is given for water and the ordinary can be transformed into the glorious. This is a direct revelation of God, not through any messenger any longer. In John the personification of the revelation of God is definite, complete, and intelligible; God, who according to Philo, is the sum of all divine activity in the world.

There is the perceived notion of the intrinsic grace and power of the Christian gospel to transform the unjust structures of human civilisation, and to redeem itself where once it colluded with the powers of empire and earthly glory to transform by imperial and colonial subjugation, conquest, and domination, which Christianity at first urged Europe into modernity in its culture, technology, and general ethos. At once, here, the Church is both in the physical earthly realm as well as under the reign of God, and there has always been tension between the two for dominance. Johann-Baptist Metz makes the observation that there is an unbiblical witness by Christianity to the gospel message that so permeates its ethos that it has become the intolerant mode of propagating the faith even in the modern era, and is the very reason that the Christian faith looks and feels alien to the landscape and cultural background of the indigenous Americas (1).

The wine of the Christian gospel was turned into vinegar and used to maintain the feudal economic and racial ascendancy of Europeans over their slaves in church and secular society because of its moral exhortations to a proper Christian lifestyle of obedience to law, the authorities, or as noted earlier, a distortion of those passages relating to the obedience of slaves to masters. Karl Marx would later define it in his age transcending statement of religion as the 'opiate of the people'; a drug, like strong wine, to deaden the effects of inhumanity and abuse on the subjugated by focussing their desires and prayers on the afterlife where in the presence of God there is perfect freedom and release. In the meanwhile, one had to endure the harsh conditions of the earthly secular order because that was the state into which one was predestined to be born, and could not change until death if one were a faithful Christian. The enslaved would be calmed and swayed away from any inclination to rebel and made to do their duty faithfully, then in heaven where there is truly no distinction, God will order our wills and conditions in a purely utopian experience. Perhaps those in ascendancy believed their mindsets would be divinely changed to allow for such revolutionary reordering of the social stratum or there might even be a continuation of the earthly order. In the preaching of the first Presbyterian missionary to Trinidad, Rev'd. Alexander Kennedy, he was said to handle the issue of slavery "without gloves".

As the president of the local arm of the Anti-Slavery Society headquartered in his Greyfriars' Church, this was evidenced by the condemnation of Kennedy's Emancipation Day sermon in the Port-of-Spain Gazette, which further preposterously attempted to demarcate the boundaries of a minister's calling. "To incite his hearers to the practice of the different duties of morality and religion – refraining from controversy on those doubtful or disputed points which will ever divide mankind, and above all, seizing no occasion or pretext to exhibit that sort of equivocal benevolence which consists in telling one part of the community that they owe no obligation, and consequently no gratitude, to the other part; to incite his hearers, we repeat, to the practice of the different duties of morality and religion, the great object of all creeds, and to refrain from observations tending to weaken them, is the only duty of a preacher, which will meet with general approval in the nineteenth century. We dismiss the subject, not without hope that we should be compelled to return to it again." (2). A good preacher will not 'rock the boat' or 'trouble the waters', but 'knowing where his bread is buttered', will ever seek to soothe his hearers with the finer, softer points of Christian duty even if society rots all around him. One's business is within the sphere of the church, and society's business is that of those who are not called to religion. Somehow the realities of the latter did not impinge on the former whose primary concern was that only of the afterlife!

There is much evidence of this thinking in the African American spirituals composed during this era, such as, "I never get weary yet, I never get weary yet; forty long years I working in the field and I never get weary yet." Of a different but similar genre are the following, "I got shoes, you got shoes, all God's chillun got shoes. When I get to heaven gonna put on my shoes; gonna walk all over God's heaven;" or this, "I got a robe up inna the kingdom, ain't a that good news. I got a crown, a seat, a harp etc. inna the kingdom;" and the classic, "Deep river, my home is over Jordan; deep river, Lord, I want to cross over into campground. Oh don't you want to go to that gospel feast, that Promised Land where all is peace." The idea here being that one should not worry about provision of material needs on earth, in heaven God will supply all, so wait until heaven. There is also the sense of hopelessness of attaining any peace of mind, body or soul because of the extent of abuses, the force of domination, and the seeming inadequacy of a gospel that calls for patience, endurance and glorying in tribulations when one sang, "Nobody knows the trouble I see;" or, "I couldn't hear nobody pray, way down yonder by myself." Professor Selwyn Cudjoe writes of Maria Jones, "Although her master possesses several valuable plantations she affirms that, "I more rich than he for al[l] that; he poor blind bukra sinner, while Fader made me rich for ever." (3). Cudjoe analyses the situation thus, "The idea that the slave was happy once s/he possessed the Lord and could sneer at the riches of the planter, is one of the tropes of this genre of fiction... The same is true of 'Daniel', a narrative similar in composition and phrasing to 'Maria Jones'. Daniel, an old African slave who lived on the same plantation as Jones and whom Rev. Cowen, pioneer London Baptist missionary to Trinidad, also befriended, utters sentiments similar to those of Jones on the death of their masters: "A short time before Daniel was called home, his owner... died suddenly, and though wealthy, he left this world poor, and miserable, and wretched, and blind, and naked. Daniel remarked when he heard of the event, 'he no rich yonder; ah, he poor, he poor!'" (4)

The economic disadvantages of colonialism perpetuated feudalism with racist discriminatory elements and entrenched peasantry with little scope for social mobility because of deliberate political and economic propaganda to these ends, have created city slums which have adopted the term, 'ghettos'. But unlike Jewish economic ingenuity which has made Jewish ghetto life mainly the name whereby their part of the city was called, Afro-Caribbean ghetto life produces gangs and gang warfare, drug mafias, crime, violence, malnutrition, squatting and, landlessness. Large families lead to a preponderance of paternal absenteeism and parents going abroad to seek a proper living, leaving children at home with physically weakened grandparents, especially grandmothers unable to give proper discipline to growing children; 'Barrel children'; who grow up without parental affinity and are only accustomed to receiving the barrels of goodies that their parents ship to them every so often. This perpetuates a vicious cycle of children with little or no education becoming involved in gangs, violence and drugs, fired with a lust for 'bling' (5).

There is little wonder that with such a socio-economic system prejudiced against them that there is no concept or feeling of belonging or ownership. This does seem a strange and unfriendly place, especially where the economies of small developing though independent nations remain subjugated to larger ones that determine and manipulate the value of world trade in goods and services to their own advantage, to maintain the colonial legacy of economic ascendancy, albeit without the dependency syndrome. These smaller nations are forced to, 'swim with the sharks', as it were, and suffer the consequences. Therefore, the system, or the 'shitstem' or' shituation' as Reggae musician Peter Tosh referred to it (6), is 'Babylonish'. And like the African American spirituals of the slave era, Reggae music and 'conscious' lyrics have taken up a prophetic role in attacking 'Babylon' and demanding individual and societal change and liberation, and in some sections, repatriation to Africa.

The songs also hint at the vicious cycle of 'Babylon' that perpetuates subsequent generations in the mess of illiteracy and eventual jail; as if by building more 'penitentiaries', the 'system' prophesies more jail and only jail for the ghetto dwellers. Bob Marley's classic, 'Redemption Song' is a clarion call for his people to re-educate themselves by the truth of African selfhood, supported by a non-White reinterpretation of the Bible, and erase the entrenched 'opiate gospel' perpetuated by 'brainwashed' Black churches and preachers who are too embedded in the 'system' to remove themselves and the socio-politico-economic who have a similar fate as the Black preachers and churches in their particular sphere of the 'system'.

It would also be this grace that would be used by the enslaved communities and their generations that came after emancipation with the clamour for nationhood, to transform the 'opiate gospel' into one of Hope, because "God will make a way somehow, where there seems to be no way". The religious opium became a powerful secret weapon in the African's fight against the evils of the imperial system, the weapon of hope. African Methodist Episcopal (AME) Bishop, Frederick Talbot, deduces that this hope is garnered through what he calls, 'Black Preaching", which was primarily the prophetic voice of a movement such as his which broke away from the White-dominated Methodist Church in the United States and ultimately from the 'pie-in-the-sky-when-you-die' opiate that they were being given. The intimate relationship with the enslaved African in one's subjugation and that of Israel in her various experiences of bondage, captivity, and exile is found among the AME, Spiritual Baptist, and other such African-influenced Christian communities, and in congregational names that reflect the very landscape of Israel, "Bethel, Mt. Zion, Mt. Carmel etc." denoting identification as God's special children. "It is through Black preaching that the lofty metaphors of God and Jesus Christ are repeated as 'realised eschatology'...[Slaves] on the plantations sang their way to sanity and psychic health. Historically, singing in the Black tradition is a 'sine qua non' of the worship experience...But it is singing together that helps to reaffirm a common bond of people who experience suffering, oppression, and yet hope and community...[Dietrich] Bonhoeffer (the great German theologian who was later to oppose Hitler and his Nazis, land in prison, and be killed for his act of courage), must have believed that this

African American spiritual, (Swing Low, Sweet Chariot), which seems to suggest escaping from this world, and used by so many interpreters as the quintessential 'otherworldly' spiritual, had another meaning...of hope and 'divine fulfilment' in history in the spirituals." (7).

This saving grace of the gospel of hope has also been instrumental in rescuing the East Indian community from total denigration and ostracism by the rest of the national community, through the efforts of the Canadian Presbyterian missionaries primarily. By establishing missions and schools specifically for this community and allowing the use of Hindi and Urdu and Indian musical instruments in their liturgy and various publications, the church gave unprecedented validity to the selfhood of this group. It also gave them, individually and communally, a sense of human dignity and value by virtue of baptism that was not allowed under the dehumanising indentureship system. (8)

It is the humble pursuit of righteous action in the face of this cosmic battle between good and evil that ushers in the new world order; not violence and hatred, not unlike the enslaved peoples who transformed the 'opiate gospel' or rather the gospel's potential for and commendation as an opiate, for the ever-powerful, undying spirit of Hope, Justice, and Liberation. The continual cleaving of the Caribbean Church has been one involving a process of dialogue and engagement with other faith-based communities which would allow for more effective ministry to the total community, in view of sharing the divine plan of creating a new and redeemed humanity under the reign of God, recognising that there are societal problems and colonial legacies that challenge everyone regardless; a continual transforming of stagnant waters into the best wine until human civilisation reflects God's glory and resembles his image, through the divine activity of the Word dwelling among us as one of us and manifesting his glory.

NOTES
1. Johan-Baptist Metz, Unity and Diversity: Problems and Prospects for Inculturation, pg. 80/2, published in World Catechism or Inculturation;

Johan=-Baptist Metz and Edward Schillebeekx, Edinburgh, T and T Clark Ltd. 1989
2. 57.   Port-of-Spain Gazette, editorial, August 3, 1838.
3. Selwyn Cudjoe, Beyond Boundaries: The Intellectual Tradition in Nineteenth-Century Trinidad, ch. 5, The Jammetization of the Culture 1838-1851, pg. 102: Calaloux Publications © 2003.
4. ibid.
5. Religion, Culture and Tradition in the Caribbean, Edited: Gossai and Murrel: J. Richard Middleton, ch. 9, Identity and Subversion in Babylon – Strategies for Resisting Against the System in the Music of Bob Marley and the Wailers: R. R. Donnelly, Harrisonburg, VA, USA, © 2000.
6. ibid.
7. Frederick Hilborn Talbot, African American Worship – New Eyes for Seeing, ch. 3, Towards a Theology of Worship – Human Responses to Divine Encounters; Preaching, pp. 69, 71; © 1998.
8. Idris Hamid, A History of the Presbyterian Church in Trinidad 1868-1968, ch. 4, The struggle for selfhood, pg. 141, © 1980.

THE SECOND SIGN

THE HEALING OF THE PARALYTIC BY THE POOL OF BETHESDA – JOHN 5

This episode is not specifically referred to as a sign. It may be described as a 'work' when Jesus uses the reference to his and his Father's working in 5: 17. However, there is a reference to the religious leaders being selective in their acceptance or rejection of evidences of the glory of God in verse 44.

Here is a man unable to walk and lying by these porticoes for 38 years. In all that time no one sought even once to help him. They helped themselves and their own. It is a testament to the utter selfishness and uncaringness of human beings to one another, outwardly religious but lacking in justice, mercy, and compassion. Thirty-eight years of being in the same place, with no advancement, and practically helpless is a harking back to Israel's 38 years in the Wilderness of Kadesh (Deut. 2:14). The thesis here can be taken from Jn 1: 17, viz. "The law indeed was given through Moses; grace and truth came through Jesus Christ." Sub-themes will include the Son of Man as Apprentice of the Father, Judge of the Resurrection, and Lord of the Sabbath.

According to our thesis, it was right and fitting in the eyes of the Jews to leave the man alone there at the pool and not venture to help him because this was most probably God's will for him. The Law of Sin and Consequences in Deuteronomy, particularly 28: 15-68, held that this man most probably had offended God's holy law in some part and was paying the consequences of his actions, therefore, he was not to be helped until the full penalty was paid, which would be seen in his healing if God so willed. But grace and truth came through Jesus Christ. Jesus comes up to the man and sets him free to walk again. He asks no question about his past or his actions, imposes no penalty, neither make any demand upon him save one question as to if he wanted to be made well. This is what Grace does. It is contrary to the Law of Sin and Consequences. It usurps the judgement of God with undeserved favour. To the Son of Man has been given all judgement by the Father, and this harmonises with his statement in Jn. 3:17, that he did not come into the world to condemn the world but to save it rather. He is therefore The Righteous Judge. The trumpet sounds and the dead in their memorial tombs are raised to life eternal by grace and forgiveness. There appears here to be a reference to the trumpet blast on the last day when the dead shall be raised and thus to the feast of trumpets in Leviticus 23, announcing the Day of Atonement and the final cycle of festivals for the calendar year. It is an announcement of the impending consummation of the reign of God begun in the Christ Event and happening at that time before their very eyes. Our revelation is, therefore, eschatological, i.e., waiting for the dawning of the perfect day when Christ and the reign or kingdom of God are revealed in all awaited and anticipated fulness.

John is mindful to point out in vs. 10 that the healing took place specifically on the Sabbath, thus bringing the thesis into question. How could God who gave a command to rest on the Sabbath have works performed in his name at that time? Jesus' answer is that the Father does not rest on the Sabbath as humans do, and neither does creation. Nature still operates, the earth turns bringing day and night, women give birth, infant boys are circumcised if the eighth day falls on a Sabbath, and many other things are kept in motion. Being thus defeated in their argument, the leaders then turn to creating another fault by which to condemn Jesus, namely that he was calling God his Father thereby making himself equal with God, a blasphemous declaration worthy of nothing less than death. He is the apprentice son and only does what he sees the Father doing, in this case showing mercy and steadfast love to a child of Abraham, and has full authority as God's presence on earth, and by associating his ministry with the work of the heavenly Father he is thereby identifying with God's saving acts in history and extending them into his time and space, as if to say, God is here among us in this person and work of Jesus.

The religious leaders were following the Law of Moses to the last jot and tittle, with its Law of Sin and Consequences. There was no room for mercy only judgement, and yet the one to whom life and judgement have been given does not use it to condemn but to save. If they were truly following the Law of Moses, they would have seen in the fulfilment of Mosaic prophecy and the laws and ordinances that he, Jesus, was manifesting his glory among them. If we truly search the scriptures and learn from what the Word says within them, rightly interpreted, we will find the full revelation of God.

Scripture presents the salvific acts of God as mystery and given to us by grace. And we perceive them and make them our own by faith. We forget salvation by grace and put in its place salvation by adhering to every word in the Bible or the Law of Moses, or salvation by holding a doctrinal position above and beyond someone else's, who is just as fallible as we are. We should rather, simply adore the Mystery, instead of seeking to analyse and find a rational explanation for it and use it to heal and create humanity anew instead of divide and condemn. How does God save a person? One does not really know. It happens differently to each person according to one's individual make-up and experiences. The healing of the paralytic at the Pool of Bethzatha / Bethesda is condemned, not only for being on the Sabbath but for Jesus' appointing himself Judge in the Father's name and healing the man without imputing any penalty! The same goes for the forgiving of the woman caught in adultery, Jn. 8: 1-11. We are saved by Grace and how it or any of the works of God happens, is Mystery. And we should be content to leave it there. To attempt to posit salvation by a belief in the way it works, as we have been doing, would be idolatrous, according to the biblical witness, for we make it contingent upon us rather than upon God.

In all of his healing miracles on the Sabbath, Jesus is seen restoring the day to its original intent and purpose – a day of liberation. Coming out as slaves from Egypt the day was given primarily as a reminder that human life does not consist of work alone; we are not robots or other machines. It was a reminder above all not to be oppressive to others in return in any way whatsoever but rather seek the liberation of others as fully integrated human beings, as per Isaiah 58: 6-14. Leonardo Boff has as his thesis that new evangelism must be done under the banner of liberation so that a truly [Latin American] Christianity, freed from colonialism, will have multi-cultural and multi-ethnic colours and shapes reflective of the Latin American landscape (1) The masses of our Caribbean people have been engaged in a struggle for selfhood and freedom over and against centuries of slavery, indentured labour, and imperialist domination. Self-determination was achieved with the granting of independence; however, it has not brought with it, in certain respects, that understanding of belonging to the land. There is still a psychic connection to the lands of our forebears, whether found in Africa, India, China, the Middle East, or Europe and a desire to belong there rather than here. For instance, Trinidadianness particularly is seen merely in terms of citizenship and not in culture and ways of being.

A legend of the First Peoples of these parts tells of the Fountain of Youth, which like our Bethesda Pool, has healing properties and the ability to sustain life in all its youthful prime for as long as one can access its waters. This eternal spring supposedly flowed somewhere in the regions of Florida, in the modern United States of America. These stories, like that of El Dorado the city of gold ruled by the Gilded One, fuelled the lust and greed of the empire builders and conquistadores, and, in their quest for this city, and this eternal spring of living water, John 7: 38, Rev. 7: 17 [both these texts having come from a common theme of the same writer], like the holy grail legends before them, they left death, destruction, domination, and every imaginable type of evil and havoc upon the land and its people in their trail; having thus demonised the landscape. Post-colonial society too has not altogether shed the remnants of Empire, but although it might have put on new garments, still holds on to the rags of its former masters in many regards. The modern quest for economic enterprise, wealth, and power is everywhere to be seen. There is also the concomitant seeking after secular materialism, and education but no wholeness of self, family life, community spirit or nationhood. It is a total quest for self-attainment, a seeking to get but not to be! In this new empire, the neo-colonialist mindset desires the gift, never the giver, the gold but not the Gilded One. As with some pseudo-Christian religions that purport to offer eternal life as a paradise on earth with every imaginable materialistic blessing to comfort us and make life as blissful as possible but with no beatific vision nor presence of God [which is reserved only for a chosen few]. These fail to realise that it is this very Life itself that sustains our life in heaven, not earthliness. What is heaven without God! What is the gift without the Giver! What is eternal life if not the very presence of the eternal God dwelling with and among his people! Paul Tillich surmises, "[The] ultimate concern with success and with social standing and with economic power. It is the goal of many people in the highly competitive Western culture, and it does what every other ultimate concern must do: it demands unconditional surrender to its laws even if the price is the sacrifice of genuine human relations, personal conviction and creative eros. Its threat is social and economic defeat and its promise – indefinite as all such promises – the fulfilment of one's being" (2). And V.S. Naipaul puts it quite succinctly, calling it, "Bongo paradise!" (3).

The dominant result of European colonisation has been the effect of Westernisation to the point that the majority of English-speaking Caribbean countries are still tied to the British monarchy, and that we are at pains to fully express who we are or want to be. From peoples whose cultural identity has been robbed or suppressed to the point of being unrecognisable as a distinct whole, people who have been taught to hate themselves and how they look, and to despise whatever they produce because Europe and North America are always far superior, we are at pains to discover and evolve into who we truly are and meant to be. The calypsonian, the Mighty Duke sang, "Black is beautiful, / Man sing it aloud! / Black is beautiful, / Say, I'm black and proud." (4). In this way, having a security of being and selfhood safely anchored within one's psyche, one would be able to move with freer access within the dominant Western order. Yet despite whatever its outward mutation, the grace of the gospel would remain faithful to its intrinsic and enduring prophetic quality and never adopt the language of empire. It is this grace of the gospel, sung as the people's new song in a foreign land that conveys a message of liberating distorted relationships based on narrow provincialism. The cosmotheandric experience can have a negative effect where human beings become too attached to land and ancestral blood ties. Here the gospel has a critical role to play by being a liberating message to the dynamic organic view of being.

To the extent that this vision has already been caught by the contextual theology of South American Christianity, both Roman Catholic and Reformed, liturgical resources were produced to be used at the Third Encounter of Bishops and Pastors from Latin America and the Caribbean held in Rio de Janeiro, Brazil in July 1993. The conference entitled, 'Seeing the Situation, Listening to Hope', produced the following song that is in tandem with the vision now being caught among Caribbean contextual theologians. It is here reproduced by this writer in his own English translation which seeks to be faithful to the original intent of the composer and to the music to which it was originally set in Spanish and Portuguese, than what was originally proffered at the then conference.

"I venture to walk around the cosmic girdle of the South
Standing in the verdant region of the wind and the light;
Sensing as I walk, the skin of all America on mine,
And through my blood, a river flows that looses its flow in my voice.

Upper Peru's Sun, Bolivia's face, ah, rust and loneliness;
Lush and green Brazil kisses my bronzed and mineral Chile,
Rising from the South towards the strange and whole America,
The pure root of a cry that's destined to emerge and fill the land.

All of the voices, all of them;
All of the hands together;
All of our blood can be a song in the wind, in the wind.
Sing out together with me;
Sing out, America's children;
Set free your hope rejoicing, raising your voice on high!" (5)

The trademark of God can be seen in all that Jesus does. Israel first knew God as Liberator in the Exodus. Our enslaved forebears identified with Israel in their enslavement and were able to transform the opiate gospel given to them by their dominators to keep them in line, into a gospel of hope, justice, selfhood, and freedom. The former paralytic was set free, liberated from all that kept him bound; free to walk, free to embark upon all he could desire to be and become, a process towards full selfhood and self-determination. Believing in Jesus is not a matter of assenting to certain doctrinal truths but of trusting the One who tells us that the truth will set us free. Indeed, whom the Son of Man sets free is free indeed (Jn. 8: 36).

The ultimate destiny of the 'oikoumene' is one of being in free and unrestrained communion with the Divine, whose presence sustains life and fulfils every pure and holy desire of the worshipper. Even this would be abused by many who seek to flatter the Almighty with vain words of adoration, seeking only his blessings of material and earthly advancement. It was Jesus' radical teaching that showed that God's favour is not manifested only in those that are successful in the eyes of the world, but the kingdom or reign of God is found in one's heart regardless of the outward situation. And so, while poverty or any kind of suffering is not acceptable, is it also not a gauge whereby judgement is cast upon those anointed by God or not. Neither is heaven for a select few chosen only by the time and era of their birth, which in some manner makes them more qualified for divine favour as if God would regard such a mere happening as the chief pivot on which his judgement stands and not the more fundamental issue of his redeeming grace.

NOTES:
1. Leonardo Boff, A New Evangelization: Perspective of the Oppressed: Pertopolis Vozes, 1990; quoted by Sherron George Op. Cit. pg. 41.
2. Paul Tillich, The Dynamics of Faith, ch. 1 What is Faith, pg. 3, Harper and Brothers, New York, N. Y. USA. 1957.
3. Banyan Ltd., Extract of a Seminar with V. S. Naipaul, Fatima College – Mucurapo, Port-of-Spain, 1974: www.pancaribbean/banyan/naipaul.htm
4. Mighty Duke (Kelvin Pope), Black is Beautiful 1969, chorus.
5. Salmos Latino Americanos {Latin American Psalm), Paulinas S.P. Brasil, published in Seeing the Situation, Listening to Hope, Liturgical Resources for Worship at the 3rd Encounter of Bishops and Pastors from Latin America and the Caribbean, Rio de Janeiro 1993, Psalm of Indigenous Peoples, song by A. Tejada Gomez and C. Sella, "Salgo a Caminar", pg. 13.

THE THIRD SIGN

THE FEEDING OF THE FIVE THOUSAND – JOHN 6
"When the people saw the sign that he had done…" Jn. 6: 14

The feeding of the five thousand with five loaves and two fish is not unique to John. However, John expands this experience into a sign of the glory of God, and in the absence of any particular institution of the Eucharist, this passage is turned into an acted parable of Jesus, the Bread of Life, and discourse on eating food that brings eternal life; in other words, eating the alternative to the fruit of the Tree of the Knowledge of Good and Evil.

Eating and drinking are as essential to life as breathing and sleeping. It is not surprising that the crowds followed Jesus for days afterwards; most probably poor, hungry, starving, oppressed masses who did not know where their next meal would come from. While not wanting to spiritualise their plight and dismiss their need for physical food, Jesus transforms the episode into a teaching moment on the meaning of mission. The mission of God, *missio Dei,* from the foundation of the world, is taken up by Christ in time and space, *missio Christi,* and extended through history in the work of the Church, *missio ecclesiae.*

Has it not been noticed that everything we eat is dead? Even if we say we are vegetarian or vegan, even fruits and vegetables die before or during the eating process. So, Jesus gives the exhortation in vs. 27 not to labour for the food that is dead and can only sustain bodily life for a short period of time but to seek after the alternative to the fruit of the Tree of the Knowledge of Good and Evil, i.e., the fruit of the Tree of Life. Using the allegory of the Garden of Eden story where the first human pair were cast out for eating in disobedience to God's command, Jesus declares in vs. 37 that anyone who now comes to him he will not drive away or cast out. In describing his flesh and blood as true and real meat and drink, he is in fact saying that his body is the fruit of the Tree of Life, metaphorically transplanted from the Garden of Eden onto the Cross of Calvary. It is not the dead flesh of an animal that one consumes but the living body of the

Lord, and thus one may eat and never die. The thesis of this sign thus finds root in Jn. 1: 12-13, viz. "But to all who received him, who believed in his name, he gave power to become children of God, 13 who were born, not of blood or of the will of the flesh or of the will of man, but of God." This metaphor can be found in the great Pange Lingua hymn of Holy Thursday by Venantius Fortunatus, "Sing my tongue, how glorious battle…" in verse 4 viz. "Faithful cross! above all other, / one and only noble tree! / None in foliage, none in blossom, / none in fruit thy peer may be: / sweet the wood and sweet the iron! / and thy load how sweet is he!" (1)

Immediately the problem arises as in vs. 52, "The Jews then disputed among themselves, saying, "How can this man give us his flesh to eat?" And many became offended, left him and followed no longer. This can be seen in his use of the noun *sarx* to denote his physical flesh and the verb *trogon* which denotes to chew, gnaw or masticate. These are vastly different from the noun used in the Synoptics at the Last Supper for his body, *soma,* and to eat, the generic verb *phagein*. The Jews are scandalised because this is the antithesis of their strict religious dietary laws. It sounds and appears cannibalistic! How would Jesus provide the synthesis for such a problem? He again turns a potentially explosive situation to his advantage, using it to weed out those who become easily offended and those who will follow faithfully to the end.

For Jesus here, faith is essential to eating the food that gives eternal life, but faith alone is not enough. Faith union and communion are what is alluded to in this verse 56. It is called in the Greek, *perichoresis,* the indwelling, where God comes to live not just with but in the believer, in heart and mind and to guide, shape, influence, and conform one's thoughts and actions to the will of God. It is a mutual indwelling and exchange of life that finds an echo in Jn 15 with the analogy of the Vine and the Branches. "Those who eat my flesh and drink my blood abide in me, and I in them," vs. 56. To chew on or masticate his flesh and fully absorb the life it offers into one's being is quite literally to go out on mission. It reads in vs. 57, "Just as the living Father sent me, and I live because of the Father, so whoever eats me will live because of me." The word mission comes from the Latin verb *mittere* from which we get the noun as used above, *missio*. The Koine Greek verb is *apostoleo,* and the Church is an apostolic church because it is 'sent' in every age and place to proclaim the Lord Jesus and to extend his work in time until the end; an eschatological community of faith and the Body of Christ. In the Early Church an unconverted person may attend a church service but only up to the point of the sermon. After the sermon the deacon would declare three times, "Catechumens depart!" And all unbaptised persons and those in training for baptism, i.e., Catechumens would have to leave. The Communion part of the service was reserved for the baptised alone. In Latin, the deacon would pronounce, "Ite, missa est!" or "Go, it is the dismissal!" Thus, the Communion rite became known as The Dismissal which morphed into Missal and later Mass. The service book used in the Communion liturgy is also called a Missal.

Hence the call to go out on mission is ever around us. Every Sunday the Body of Christ is 'dismissed', scattered into the world on mission, as individuals, sent, as it were, to perform their service after the Service, or as the Eastern Orthodox would say, your liturgy after the Liturgy. And principally on Sunday, though at other times too, the Church is gathered again to be renewed and refilled before being sent out again. This gathering in English, we call remembrance, in obedience to the Lord's sacramental command, "Do this in remembrance of me." But only in English can we say that the scattered Body of Christ is "re-membered" Sunday by Sunday, and whenever else the scattered members come back into one whole. Thus, to be 'dismissed' means to be 'sent out', and the church is sent out as the people of God bearing Good News to evangelise the world, to live and commend the life of this kingdom which they experience in worship. This is the normal trend of biblical revelation. The experience of the Christ Event brings into being a new economy, 'oikonomia', in the sphere of the reign of God, and Christian worship pre-eminently forms part of this new economy.

The mission of the Church has been the subject of many a church conference in all times, places, and denominations. The Church must ever keep abreast of changing times and trends. As Charles Wesley would put it, "To serve the present age / My calling to fulfil; / O may it all my powers engage / To do the Maser's will!" (2). Yet very often the Church has confused this missiological appeal with the final realisation of the reign of God which has not yet come. While the Church is A kingdom of sorts ruled by Christ the King, it is not THE Kingdom but rather an agent of the Kingdom of God and at its service. This confusion of roles has led to a triumphalist approach to mission that has seen the denigration, conquest, subjugation, and destruction of peoples and cultures in an attempt to assert Western Christianity as the all-conquering, over-arching Truth of all ages.

The biblical witness, however, was one where, "...acknowledgement of and engagement with others in their otherness was central." (3). This was the pattern of early Judaism in its Semitic, Babylo-Persian and Egyptian surroundings. This was the apostolic pattern of the New Testament Church as it encountered Greco-Roman thought, culture and religious cults. This was the pattern of the Early Church, from Celtic Britain to the Copts of North Africa, as it became the official religion of the Roman Empire. Celtic spirituality is now being recovered and more widely appreciated and it was his encounter with this experience that has led the author to seek to develop a model along similar lines within one's native context. This has become the pattern of younger Churches such as Christianity in Latin America, Africa, and New Zealand and its encounter with the Maori experience. But the Christianity that came to these shores was not the apostolic model of engagement and encounter, rather it was the triumphalist model of a religion married to the empire. Seeing that Christianity became synonymous with Europeanisation and that one cannot strip modern Caribbean and Latin-American Christianity from its European garments without doing fundamental damage to its essence, what needs to be done is to have it stripped rather of its excess baggage namely; its Western imperialist, intolerant triumphalism that saw the devil in everything and everyone that was not Christian and the capacity to dehumanise and despise the 'otherness of others'; seeing that this is the level Christianity attained when it was brought here, and to seek to reinterpret the apostolic model to suit the present society as it has become through the turbulent experience of the past.

The Church is but an agent of mission in the unity of the faith and a sign of God's reign in humanity's midst; one which has the capacity to make the 'other' feel at home. The church will then be rid of the triumphalist tone with which, till now, it has been using to speak the language of empire to preach an opiate gospel, and commend itself and a sanitised gospel in joyful penitence, humble service, and glad obedience. There is therefore a need for the reciprocal sharing of cultures as bridge builders in the church. A viable contextual strategy should simultaneously accommodate traditional forms and values, reinterpret them in the light of Christian theology and ethics, and innovate forms which are consistent with biblical faith, the Trinbagonian / Caribbean / New World cultural heritage, and emerging social values. In so doing, the Caribbean Church can express its cultural loyalty, maintain biblical integrity, and pursue the transformational goal of contextualisation.

There is also the need to acknowledge that the gospel transcends all cultures and that in any event, all cultures need the gospel. The prophetic grace of the gospel must be allowed to critique and baptise the culture and local landscape, thus bringing it into the new and redeemed order of creation; through identification with the person and work of Christ, by removing those things that are foreign to justice, joy, mutual edification, compassion, peace, beauty, and order. In his incarnation, Jesus is the Word made Flesh and dwelling among us, not in some far-off distant land and in another time and era but in the here and now, in our time and space, in our neighbourhood, and in true and tangible flesh and blood indeed, as this sign is teaching us to recognise him. And it is within this faith experience that the church must ever guard against spiritualising the Gospel away from the people's lived experience, especially that of pain and suffering. As the mystic Body of Christ, extending the incarnation of God into this present day and age, the church is called to express in tangible and practical ways its solidarity with those who suffer in any way and commend to them living hope for liberation and not the 'pie-in-the-sky-when-you-die' colonial model of an opiate gospel. It was real bread and fish that were blessed, multiplied, and shared to hungry masses, and not a word for their souls alone; and it was real flesh and blood he was commending of himself for the life of the world.

Within this experience of the living Word of God in real, tangible, edible human flesh and blood, the church as a whole but the Reformed tradition particularly, needs to affirm all of creation as intrinsically good, thus endowed by its Creator God, and to encourage the doctrine of all of nature, therefore, as a sacrament, because God has used various elements of it for his sovereign purpose; even things that would normally be classed as evil or unholy and defiled, such as the brazen serpent as a sacramental channel of healing and grace in Numbers 21: 9, or Jesus' use of saliva to cure the blind man's eyes in Jn. 9: 6, and others as Mary the Mother of God, the burning bush, shepherds, a stable, animal sacrifice, bread, wine, water, oil, salt, words, and a host of others. "You are worthy, our Lord and God, to receive glory and honour and power, for you created all things, and by your will [for thy pleasure, KJV], they existed and were created." Rev. 4: 11. The Reformed along with the rest of the Christian church must avow the doctrine of the Right Use of Creation since all can be used for good or for ill. The same sacramental brazen serpent was later idolatrously worshipped by the Israelites and had to be destroyed, 2 Kgs. 18: 4. This understanding makes for a reversal of the traditional imperialist views of the created order as rational and instrumental. Did not God give humanity 'dominion over the earth'? Is not the land, the air and the sea with all their resources at the disposal of humankind's every need, i.e., to serve humanity, but which has been exploited and plundered by insatiable lust and greed? The old patriarchal colonial powers were guilty of regarding the land as an empty, dead, feminine-like thing to be conquered and subjugated.

God's redemption of humankind in Jesus Christ is not limited to people, nor is it completed in it. It is a continuing process that involves the whole created order or cosmos; the physical/material, the moral/ethical, cultural, political, social, economic, and religious; in other words, a total interconnectedness of all states of being and doing. An ancient Eucharistic liturgy symbolises this dynamic relationship between the death of Christ that brings forth new life and the creative forces of both nature and humanity;
"Blessed are you, Lord, God of all creation.

Through your goodness we have this bread to offer,
Which earth has given and human hands have made.
It will become for us the bread of life.
Blessed be God for ever.

Blessed are you, Lord, God of all creation.
Through your goodness we have this wine to offer,
Fruit of the vine and work of human hands.
It will become for us the cup of salvation.
Blessed be God for ever.

Blessed are you, Lord, God of all creation.
Through your goodness we have ourselves to offer,
Fruit of the womb, and formed by your love.
We will become your people for the world.
Blessed be God for ever. "(4). The prayer also implies that what is being offered is not just the actual bread, wine and people in the actual moment, but they are given as representations of the sum total of all created existence; human, natural and metaphysical: the energies of life, the struggles, being ground and crushed, burnt and bruised like wheat and grape to make bread and wine. It symbolises all of life as a search for wholeness. People desire to be fully human, with disease and disappointment as well as strength and accomplishment, hungry for bread both for stomach and soul, and be thus fully present with God and presented to God, who himself is fully present with his creation in Christ Jesus and who alone can make perfect the offering, even as this Jesus became fully human for us in all that the human experience entails…

To quote South Korean Presbyterian Pastor, Kyong Jae Kim, "The gospel cannot simply be translated from one culture to another. It needs to be embodied in the unique understanding of that community, to be in organic relationship with that culture. The human mind does not work like a plant, reacting to new soil in a physical and chemical manner. It works through understanding, through a hermeneutic 'fusion of horizons' (Gadamer}…This dynamic relationship between the gospel and cultures 'shapes' how humans understand, respond to and articulate God's revelation in Jesus Christ." (5). This embodying of the Gospel finds root in our pivot verse of John 1: 14, "And the Word became flesh and lived among us, and we have seen his glory, the glory as of a father's only son, full of grace and truth." It is also echoed in this sign here, as he gives his full corporeal presence for the attaining of eternal / resurrection / aeonian life, and further, that in eating his flesh and drinking his blood we too embody his life, mission, and witness, in the church as his Body, thus making it our own, even as regular food becomes part of our bodies, and extending it in time and space to every successive generation. The *missio Dei* which Christ embodied as *missio Christi* now becomes the *missio ecclesiae*. In his incarnation, he is the Word made Flesh and dwelling among us. In his resurrection and ascension, he becomes the cosmic overlord who is bringing all creation to the fulness of its destiny.

At this present time of writing the Church and the world are bearing the ravages of the Covid-19 pandemic, and while in many parts of the world churches are closed to regular services and liturgy, or congregational singing may be outlawed, for the time being, the *missio ecclesiae* nevertheless continues unabated though in new forms via Facebook and Whatsapp, YouTube, Instagram, and Zoom and Google Meet. The Church's missionary mandate to deliver the justice and peace of God's reign may be viewed in this regard: to shape humanity anew, in Christ as head and us as body; in Christ to redirect all humanity's dreams and aspirations back to their desired fulfilment in God, and finally, to unite all things, heavenly and earthly, under his eternal and sublime Lordship even as he is united as divine and human in one Person. It is this vision of the new, re-created humanity that has prompted the Church to be uniquely involved in a universal mission. The possibility of the new humanity has taken shape historically in the Church with its various supporting ecclesiastical structures and is meant only as a foretaste of the final reality.

NOTE:
1. Venantius Honorius Fortunatus, 540?-600? AD, "Pange lingua gloriosi proelium certaminis" verse 4
2. Charles Wesley 1707-1788, A charge to keep I have, verse 2

3. Johan-Baptist Metz, Unity and Diversity: Problems and Prospects for Inculturation, pg. 80/2, published in World Catechism or Inculturation; Johan=-Baptist Metz and Edward Schillebeekx, Edinburgh, T and T Clark Ltd. 1989

4. Book of Common Order of the Church of Scotland, Prayers for use at Holy Communion, pg. 191, St. Andrew Press, Edinburgh, 1994.

5. Kyoung Jae Kim, A Northeast Asian Perspective, published in Reformed World, theological journal of the World Alliance of Reformed Churches, Geneva, Switzerland, Volume 46, No. 1, March 1996, pg.17.

THE FOURTH SIGN

THE HEALING OF THE MAN BORN BLIND – JOHN 9
"How can a man who is a sinner perform such signs?" Jn. 9: 16

In chapter 7, the Jewish authorities are still smarting from the healing of the paralytic on the Sabbath by the Pool of Bethesda. This debate among themselves as to the authenticity of Jesus and his ministry paves the way for two further acts that would cement their outrage and desire to get rid of him once and for all; in chapters 8 and 9. In this regard, these chapters 7, 8, and 9 can be said to be written in the style of the Aristotelian three-act play. Chapter 7 introduces Jesus' hiding from the Pharisees because his time has not yet come to be given over to his ultimate glory, a time he will choose. It also sees the authorities still up in arms about the paralytic's healing. The people then chime in their chorus as they debate among themselves also. Then there is the drama of the woman caught in adultery and about to be stoned to death, whom Jesus saves and forgives. Jesus then proceeds to defend the authenticity of his ministry publicly. The episode reaches a head in the healing of the man born blind, again on the Sabbath, provoking further ire and indignation. In the end, the conclusion is reached that it is spiritual blindness that causes people not to see the works of God in their midst and to miss the signs or to misread them as something they are not.

Our theme in this sign is of Jesus, the Light of the world juxtaposed against the spiritual blindness of the religious authorities, and our thesis is found in Jn. 1: 4-5, "In him was life, and the life was the light of all people. 5 The light shines in the darkness, and the darkness did not overcome it." What an astonishing thing! "Never since the world began has it been heard that anyone opened the eyes of a person born blind," vs. 32. Jesus does several things here. As with the healing of the paralytic, it was assumed that this man was also paying for his sins in his suffering and condition. The opening question by the disciples bears witness to a commonly held view that all suffering was a result of sin. We seek answers and explanations to attain clarity to things we cannot understand, thus to our inherent human blindness. Somebody had to have sinned. Our fortune or misfortune is naturally dependent on the karmic law that we pay for our deeds. And this is a universal law! Yet no one sinned, but that the glory of God might be manifested in him when Jesus heals him by his grace.

Antithetical to this are the statements and questions. This has never happened before to our knowledge! How did this happen? Who did this to you? This man is a sinner, he does not observe the Sabbath! Does God hear the prayers of sinners? The authorities are concerned not with the truth but with their material and societal interests of the legal process; how they can prevent a popular riot as a result of this man's teachings and miracles and not cause Rome any worry so as to remain securely in power.

The man's parents are called in to answer questions, but they refuse because no adult can stand proxy for another of legal age. Jesus, in declaring himself the Light of the world in Jn. 8: 12ff acknowledges that evidential witness is not what was required to prove his works but that the truth bears witness to itself. The truth of the thesis can be found in the way Jesus heals this blind man. Jesus announces in this sign that he has come to renew the face of the earth. He spits on the ground, makes moistened clay, and anoints the man's eyes and the man can see again. Spit or saliva is composed of water and breath, the two things present at the world's creation in Genesis 1, John 1: 1-3, when the Spirit hovered over the face of the waters incubating the world for the creative word to take force. He spits on the dry, dead, barren, fruitless desert earth and makes it potent to heal. He is renewing the face of creation. That barren earth recalls humanity's fruitless longings, its sin and its failures. And that makes us blind to the things of God. With the anointing of the Spirit the veil of distorted vision is removed, and we can see clearly the glory of God, unlike the Pharisees who claimed to see but were really spiritually blind. He is the Lord of nature, as with the changing of water into wine, and has come to take possession of his creation and make it full of life again. If the religious authorities were truly blind and in humility acknowledged their need of God's clarity, they would have had no sin, as per 1 Cor. 13: 9, "Our knowledge is imperfect." But because they claimed to see, their sin remained, and they condemned themselves.

The process of divine revelation takes place in time, space, and history. Religion has been culturally adapted and has used the story forms of myth and legend to convey truths about nature and natural phenomena that can now be understood by scientific verification owing to ever-growing advancements in technology. T. F. Torrance writes, "Because Revelation meets us in the creaturely reality of our fallen world, it conceals Christ behind Proclamation and Sacrament as well as reveals him. It is of the nature of mystery manifest in the flesh." 1 Tim. 3: 16, cf 3: 9; Eph. 1: 9, 3: 3f, 6: 19; Col. 1: 26ff, 2: 2, 4: 3 etc. ...So long as we wait for the redemption of the body, therefore, we are forbidden to have a static condition in the Church....otherwise than in the mystery of a worldliness that is already under judgement." (1). Revelation should seek to serve the Church rather than to control it. We adhere to doctrinal positions and interpretations as if they were the finished revelation for all time, and that nothing will change or be made new ever again. We preach salvation by adherence to a particular form of doctrine; be it predestination or free will or co-operation with the grace of God. We concretise the presence of Christ in the Eucharist and any failure to accept a position of belief is cause for excommunication. We quibble over the sequence and nature of events surrounding the Second Coming. We fight as to how right and biblically correct our outward forms of worship are rather than our attitude, and fail to see that there are no set patterns or full answers given, only basic outlines.

The rest, St. Paul, said to the Corinthian church, he would have set in order when he would have come to them in person, 1 Cor. 11: 34. Suppose the Apostle did leave a fixed liturgical order and other specific guidelines that he and the apostolic college considered divinely inspired and which may be said to be continued by certain branches of the church today, but because they are in those sections of the church and also not specifically written in the Bible, they are naturally suspect to other branches and therefore spurned. We want the Bible to tell us everything, and it does not, it cannot, because it is chiefly concerned with Salvation History. Furthermore, it presents the salvific acts of God as mystery, and given to us by grace. And we perceive them and make them our own by faith. We forget salvation by grace and truth, Jn. 1: 17.

Paul Tillich holds the view that any attempt at infallibility of a decision by a council or a bishop or a book tends to the exclusion of doubt in the realm of faith, making it static. "This static faith without doubt is idolatrous since the element of doubt seeks only to confirm that it involves a risk to be taken against reason"; which risk-taking he calls 'courage'. "Courage does not need the safety of an unquestionable conviction. It includes the risk without which no creative life is possible." (2). This 'life of faith' as seen especially from the Old Testament can never be a mechanical revelation, once for all. The church has had to deal with the issues of the Jewish Sabbath, circumcision, dietary laws, levirate marriage, and a host of others. These were all given to a particular people in a particular social and geographic background, and as practised today by modern Orthodox Judaism, could never be divinely binding on all cultures and living conditions of humanity, where they find themselves logically irrelevant. It is precisely the church's present problem when it searches scripture to find answers to situations within modern contexts that are alien to the biblical landscape and timeline, as with divorce and remarriage, or the homosexuality debate. Early Church Father Justin Martyr writes, "Before the coming of Christ men had been enabled to attain to bits and pieces of the truth through the possession of 'seeds' of the Divine Reason; at Christ's coming the whole 'Logos' took shape and was made man." (3).

There exists within the mindset of the post-colonial Caribbean Church remnants of speaking with the voice of a *'theologia gloriae'*; heightened by a modern North American evangelistic tone; a language of heathens, pagans, savages, and barbarians, regarding anyone who was different. Its 'theologia gloriae' was heightened when in Europe it warded off invasion by Islamic Turks, Ottomans, Berbers, and Moors, and turned the political scenario into a religious one through the Crusades. Its triumph in the civilising of Europe made it regard itself as the one with the 'light', to be commended to those still in heathen darkness. Anyone living then would have thought and spoken that language. Indeed they thought they were faithful to biblical witness with Old Testament injunctions against idolatry and pagan religion, or any religion that was not identified with God's people, even Judaism which later refuted Jesus as the Messiah; which, in its own right, is and has been part of the general Christian ethos. Christianity saw itself as the one charged with a universal missiological mandate; to 'go into all the world' with the gospel of Jesus Christ. Armed with this Old Testament world view of a world in spiritual darkness until they receive the 'light' of the gospel, the church used the state's expansionist foreign policy to allow it to enter into lands hitherto unreachable by regular missionary means and meagre church financing.

This world view is found in the spiritual arrogance of several of the missionary hymns of the colonial era that belied the sincere piety with which they were sung and prayed, and which were laden with ideas of "plucking the heathen from their darkness", 'heathen' referring to the non-European peoples of the conquered, subjugated world. (4) In the hymn, "Hills of the north, rejoice", the world is racially and culturally divided into the four but strict cardinal points without any regard for any kind of cross-fertilisation that may have been taking place. Even when comparing the geography of these four corners, the 'north' emerges as the place to be, the lands most favoured by God and the ones charged with the spiritual, technological, and civil enlightenment of the world. The first verse refers to the 'North' or Europe, where amid peaceful and refreshing 'rivers and mountain springs', the people have been waiting long yet faithfully for their Lord's return. Verse two calls to the 'isles of the southern seas' to 'pent' their 'warring breeze' and 'lull' their 'restless waves' in view of the coming gospel that would make their 'wastes' the Lord's 'great highway'. In verse three, the 'lands of the east' must 'awake' from and 'break' their 'sleep of ages'. The gospel, which dawns on their hills 'long cold and grey' promises 'liberty' from whatever bondage they are facing; spiritual, dictatorial and any other. 'The shores of the utmost west' are considered in verse four, where in spite of the massive, ancient and comparatively advanced indigenous civilisations, they 'have waited long, unvisited, unblest'. The fifth and last verse is perhaps the only biblically faithful one and can be divorced from the rest of the hymn as being of the true essence of the gospel and the church, though it is used as its conclusion: "Shout while we journey home; / Songs be in every mouth; / Lo, from the north we come, / From east, and west, and south. / City of God, the bond are free, / We come to live and reign in thee!" (5). Although these and other like hymns were of British extract, their common denigrating theme was nonetheless one shared by European Christianity on the whole.

The late Rev. Dr. Idris Hamid of the Presbyterian Church in Trinidad surmises, "The political ethic of the church leaders was guided by a merger of two elements. On the one hand, there was Presbyterianism with its strong view on Divine Providence and the sovereignty of God: a Providence which 'has not, without good cause, arranged that different countries should be governed by different forms of policy;' and a sovereignty with its insistence that 'there is no power but of God,' with its strong call to obey and submit and its view on law and order. On the other hand was the political ethos of what one may call the political myths of the times.....One of these myths is the conviction by Western Christianity that it has a mission to schoolmaster the rest of the pagan or heathen world.....Reinforcing this myth was another closely related one, that Western political powers were beneficent and were ordinances of God, which guaranteed the propagation of the gospel and which did Christian work by its trade and through the establishment of Western institutions. There is also a messianism at work in the minds of the Western church. Their mission to evangelise was influenced more by Old Testament examples of conquest by Israel over other nations than by the suffering servant image in the Bible." (6).

Dutch Reformed missiology professor, Pieter Holtrop remarks whether Reformed theology, "...is able to take people seriously, people as they are, people already touched by grace. In other words, does Reformed theology take the doctrine of creation seriously....or must we admit that the Calvinist doctrine of grace and redemption does not have anything to do with historic reality, other than plucking people out of this' realm of darkness'? It causes Andre Karamaga (of the All Africa Conference of Churches) to question the widespread opinion, even within the mainline churches in Africa itself, that the African cultural/religious inheritance, when seen in the light of the gospel, was only to show darkness. It makes him wonder whether Reformed theology may admit that God, as known by Christians in the West, already was and is known in Africa, far before the missionary movement started witnessing to God, that Africa has its special knowledge, as the Giver and source of Life, life-in-community." (7).

This arrogance was a deeply rooted Christian theological concept and conviction that is even carried over into today's post-colonial era by many fundamentalist quarters of Christianity, Protestant, Orthodox and Roman Catholic. It is the idea that divine revelation is limited to the biblical witness alone and that the 'nations' are plunged into a spiritual ignorance, darkness, and/or distortions about God that have been the work of the devil and his evil host through the ages. Therefore, nothing in their religious experience can be trusted since they have been confused with the 'doctrine of devils' and whatever truth might be left has been clouded beyond recognition.

What about the Church's attitude today? Is there a place for the continued intolerance of the revelations of other faiths? Has the Church made Jesus Christ too final? Has our faith / religion become idolatrous in that it is prized more than God or what God is doing among other people and faith communities? For Tillich, "An idolatrous faith which gives ultimacy to a preliminary concern stands against all other preliminary concerns and excludes love between... contrasting claims. The fanatic cannot love that against which his fanaticism is directed." (8) J. Vernon Bartlet reports that both Sadducees and Pharisees were practically equal in their denial of God's progressive will and ways. (9). Hence the church's continuing enthusiasm, ever readiness, arrogance to condemn to hell all that is not decidedly Christian, in its eagerness to spread the gospel and 'win the world for Christ'.

Christianity has many stories to tell of "heathen tribes with idolatrous worship and barbarous, cannibalistic practices"; of missionaries facing the dangers of the unknown to carry the light of the gospel to those in darkness or developing written codes for new languages or translating the Bible into them; of churches, mission and Bible societies at home raising funds and being engaged in such an exotic activity as having an overseas mission and receiving back stories to tell to far and wide. But it would separate justice from justification, body from spirit, and the reign of God from any association with this present life, and ultimately lose its prophetic voice and drift more and more away from the biblical witness and apostolic model of engagement/encounter evangelism.

Validity and affirmation, intrinsic human worth and dignity of being do not come from an appraisal of one's being and work by alien thought processes and words. Neither do they depend on such foreign approbation, but rather from a self-awakening to one's having been created in the image and likeness of God, as equal as any other human being, and that the glory of God may be seen in who one is as a full human person and in the work, God can do through a person, as with this former blind man. They come also on popular acclamation among those who share a common way of seeing and being. These virtues come from a radical desire to re-educate the post-colonial generations with a sense of intrinsic self-worth of themselves and the ancient cultures and races from which they have evolved. Because they were created by God and endowed with the gift of faith. It may be that nobody sinned as in the former blind man's case, because as Henry Wilson reminds us that all good has its source in God (10), but that the glory of God would be seen when they emerge from centuries of being taught to hate themselves, of seeing nothing good in anything that they intrinsically are or can do. Calypsonian, the Mighty Duke sings, "It's quite important, simple though it seem / We have achieved what once was thought a dream / We have been imitating in the past / Now we have found our very own at last / No more hot combs to press we hair / And no more bleach creams to make us clear. / Proudly I say without pretext / No more inferiority complex / Because we know / Black is beautiful..." (11)

It involves zealousness for these virtues of self-awareness because there can be no justice without national and personal justification. It is a response to the dynamic action of the Holy Spirit who gives love and freedom, of the mysterious God who is always with, and gives true life, to all creation. (12). Kyoung Jae Kim remarks with clarity, "God enjoys and blesses the diversity of the created world and the feast of the gospel. Through the descent of the Holy Spirit on the day of Pentecost the diversity of race, culture and tradition was affirmed, and the unity in diversity experienced (Acts 2: 1-13) Diverse cultures and religious traditions are not a stumbling block to God's mission, but rather a creative challenge and opportunity to experience God's infinitude and depth of the gospel." (13). Post-colonial Caribbean Christianity must come to insist on the total salvation and dignity of every human person, seeing that here can be no justification before God without the concomitant justice here on earth

Who are you, holy, hidden Being? We glimpse you vaguely in shadows, sometimes we speculate, and make inferences, but are not really sure. We often confuse our will with yours because either we just do not know or what you say to us is not suited to our desires. We make triumphant claims to the exclusion of others', and we believe that we have it, but in the face of new challenges these claims seem irrelevant, and we are confused about right and wrong, and we confess we do not really know you or your full will for us at all times. Who are you God? The Event of Jesus Christ was a once-for-all event in human history, a definitive, once-for-all, total, and all-embracing activity of God in the human event of his person and work that brings together the divergent strands of revelation, and knowledge of God's activity on the stage of human history, both before and after, into a convergent integrity specifically aimed at a final or eschatological and culminating consummation in the glory of God

"No one has ever seen God. It is God the only Son, who is close to the Father's heart, who has made him known.
Jn. 1: 18.

NOTES:
1. T. F. Torrance, Royal Priesthood
2.. Paul Tillich, The Dynamics of Faith, 1957, Harper and Brothers, New York, N. Y. USA., chapter 1, section 6, Faith and Community pp. 28-29 and chapter 6, The life of faith, section 1, Faith and Courage, pg. 101.

3. The Early Christian Fathers, A selection from the writings of the Fathers from St. Clement of Rome to St. Athanasius, Oxford University Press, 1956/69, ed. Henry Bettenson, Introduction pg. 10.
4. William Williams, O'er Those Gloomy Hills of Darkness; Missions no. 444, The Church Hymnary 1898.
5. Hills of the North, Rejoice!, Hymns Ancient and Modern Revised no. 269, William Clowes (Beccles) Ltd. London.
6. Idris Hamid, A History of the Presbyterian Church in Trinidad 1868-1968; The
 Struggles of a Church in Colonial Captivity, ch. 4, The Struggle for Selfhood, pg129.
7. Pieter Holtrop, Mission as Life –In-Community: A Biblical Reflection, published in Reformed World, theological journal of the World Alliance of Reformed Churches, Geneva Switzerland, Volume 42, No. 2 June 1992, pg. 35.
8. Op. cit. 2
9. J. Vernon Bartlet, The Religious Background of the New Testament, Peake's Commentary on the Bible, Thomas Nelson and Sons Ltd. 1919. pg. 637.
10. Henry S. Wilson, Worship and Culture, published in Reformed World, theological journal of the World Alliance of Reformed Churches, Geneva Switzerland., Volume 41, No. 2, June 1990, pg. 61.
11. Mighty Duke (Kelvin Pope), Black is Beautiful 1969, verse 2.
12. Kyoung Jae Kim, A Northeast Asian Perspective (on Gospel and Cultures), published in Reformed World, theological journal of the World Alliance of Reformed Churches, Geneva Switzerland, Volume 46, No. 1, March 1996, pg. 19.
13. ibid.

THE FIFTH SIGN

THE RAISING OF LAZARUS – JOHN 11
"They heard that he had performed this sign..." Jn. 12: 18

The raising of Lazarus has been described as the most significant miracle of Jesus next to his own resurrection. It is set within an Old Testament context. Jesus was in Jerusalem for the Feast of Dedication or Hanukkah around the time of the winter solstice or our modern-day Christmas, according to Jn. 10: 22. He has just denounced the spiritual blindness of the religious authorities in his own healing of the man born blind, and significantly so at this time of the Festival of Lights. Faced with growing hostility against his teaching he withdraws to the Transjordan region where he stays for the next couple months of Tevet and Shevat during which time he receives the news that his friend Lazarus was gravely ill. These months signify a time of the earth's renewing as winter begins to give way to spring and crops come through the soil to the surface. Shevat, particularly, was heralded as a new year for trees.

Jesus as the Word of God, Jn. 1: 1 in the Transjordan region at that time of year, and weeks before his own passion and death, calls to mind Moses' summarising of the Law or Torah 'on the other side of the Jordan' at this same time of year and also immediately prior to his death, Deut. 1. Again here we have the juxtaposition of Law and Grace, Moses and Jesus, as per Jn 1: 17. The first day of Shevat, with its commemoration of the recitation of the Law also calls to mind the Day of Pentecost or Shavuot when the giving of the Law to Moses was celebrated, the Law recited again, and the Covenant renewed. It would be this 'Pentecostal-like' time that Jesus, through Word and Spirit calls Lazarus to life once more.

The other Old Testament context has to do with the setting of the scene in vs. 7 where Jesus invites his disciples to go with him to Judea, knowing full well the fate that awaited him there. This is the impending time of his glorification, the consummation of his life and ministry in the fullest display of the glory of God in cross and resurrection. Going into Judea to take possession of his cosmic overlordship of the whole created order, Jn. 12: 31, sees the fulfilment of Genesis 49: 10, viz. "The sceptre shall not depart from Judah, nor the ruler's staff from between his feet, until tribute comes to him." For "tribute" the King James Version renders, "Shiloh" and the exact wording has led to interminable discussion. In any event, it is a messianic reference here, most likely interpolated by later redactionists and gleaned from the prophets who built upon, contested, and refined an already extant eschatology. (1) Shiloh, or the one whose it is, has come to take possession of his messianic reign as the Lord of life. "...in him was life, and the life was the light of all people." Jn 1: 4, which is our thesis for this sign. The problem comes when the Jews murmured among themselves as Jesus wept in solidarity with the grieving sisters, "Could not he who opened the eyes of the blind man have kept this man from dying?" vs. 36

In the raising of Lazarus Jesus is proclaiming himself the one who has come to renew the whole created order. All things were made by him in the beginning, Jn. 1: 3, and the very word used to call the worlds into being is the very word that becomes flesh and dwells among us in his person. And that is the same creative word he uses to call Lazarus out of the tomb. As the Word of God from the beginning, now enfleshed as a human being in time and place, Jesus' word has creative, life-giving power. Words are formed by breath. Words are our thoughts incarnate. The same breath that breathed over the waters in the beginning and created the world, Gen. 1: 1-3a, is the same breath that was called into the bones in Ezekiel's vision to bring life again to them, Ezek. 37. That breath is the very Spirit of God, (Ruach YHWH), and Jesus was conceived of the Holy Spirit and at his baptism the Spirit descended upon him in all plenitude and power as upon no other human being, showing he was the Son of God.

In the death of Lazarus, as with every death, humankind is excluded from the glory or the presence of God. Resurrection speaks of new life, the return of the glory, the *chabod,* which had previously departed, Ezek. 37. The world stinks in death and the Covid 19 pandemic has exposed that most starkly. It is seen in the fear of the people, "Don't remove the stone! He's been dead four days. "Peradventure he stinketh!" God's Word exposes the sin but reveals grace and mercy, Jn. 1: 17. It slays the wicked, as in the Sword of the Word, 2 Thess. 2: 8, Rev. 19: 15, and it is that revelation of God's glory, his manifest presence in the face of Jesus the Son that will heal the world. As Jesus says to Mary, "Did I not tell you that if you believed, you would see the glory of God?" vs. 40. Jesus does not bring judgement and punishment to us but life everlasting. In his judgement we are not judged but rather the judgement of sin and death is reversed and the grace, mercy, and glory of God are restored.

"I am the resurrection and the life. Those who believe in me, even though they die, will live, and everyone who lives and believes in me will never die." John 11: 25-26a. Here is the reign of God in action. It is not a future reality but a present activity. I AM, not I will be! Resurrection takes place here and now. Now is the Day of the Lord, the Latter Day, the Day of Eternal Life, the Day of Salvation, indeed, the Day that the Lord has made. It is a Day that has begun with the coming of Jesus, the Christ Event and which is growing with ever continuing brightness on all the world until it reaches its high noon at the second appearing. In this declaration of being Resurrection and Life, Jesus is received as having all power and authority in heaven and on earth even over the great power of death.

For St. Paul, in the letter to the Romans, to have the mind fixed on things of the flesh is death but to set the mind on the Spirit is life and peace, Rom. 8: 1-17. Death is the ultimate separation from life and being. It is, however, this vision of God and fellowship or divine communion and intercourse with him, which he himself promises, that will sustain his people throughout eternity and fulfil their every desire. In other words the goal of heaven is not the procurement of materialistic blessings which are already humanity's aim in this earthly realm. But the goal of heaven is and must be God himself, otherwise humankind and satisfaction of one's needs become the idolatrous primary focus. Death is the wedded bride of human greed, the ultimate end of human justice, wreaking its full havoc through imperialist and modern-day conquistadors with their insatiable desire and selfish passion, their lustful, greedy, murderous intentions; seeking to plunder, destroy and exploit, to drain, milk and exhaust the riches and the leaves of the trees and the Holy Grail. And their vain longings and carnal strivings do remain agonisingly unsatisfied for all eternity. "But if the Spirit of him who raised Jesus from the dead dwells in you, he who raised Christ from the dead will give life to your mortal bodies also through his Spirit that dwells in you." Rom 8: 11.

John does not appear to have any notion of chronological time say, as with Luke who carefully measures out times and seasons, such as the time between Jesus death, resurrection, ascension, and the coming of the Holy Spirit. For John it is all one glorious Event in time with different experiences. John's time, therefore is 'chairological', if there be such a word; from the Greek, *kairos,* opportune time as against chronological time which is counted in days and hours. Revelation is not mechanical or in a vacuum, but evolving within a pattern of a lineal history towards an eventual goal / consummation, as espoused in Judaeo-Christian thought, and all of Creation becomes the *"theatrum gloriae dei,"* the theatre (place for acting out) God's glory / presence. Thus Jesus is acting out God's glory in this scene set on a stage by Lazarus' tomb. A divine drama!

Unlike the promise of new life which the Jewish months of Tevet and Shevat portend, here in the Caribbean a different scenario unfolds. At that time of year the earth is not in the thralls of a renewing creation but rather the opposite as the Dry Season presses on with its death, dryness, burning, and drought. The land is parched, hard, and dry. The hillsides are heartlessly and heedlessly slashed and burnt to make way for new farmlands but failing ever to be aware that this causes serious flooding of the lowlands when the rains come. But somehow in this land, flooding is always the government of the day's fault! The days are hot; and there is little or no rain and the rivers and streams all dry up. These images speak to us of crucifixion, pain, death, and suffering. It is the appropriate time for fasting and abstinence. Amidst the joy of the sunshine and the ability to work outdoors because it is impracticable in a torrential downpour, the lack of rain speaks of a potent threat to fertility, to food, to new birth, new life. Yet in the midst of the aridity, there is the hope and promise of the returning rain. The much expected Poui trees blossom in regal splendour, and deck the fields with resplendent colour. When the Poui blooms it is known that rain is near. And when it comes with the April showers, life can begin again. The resurrected Christ is the Church's, Returning Rain, risen to renew the face of the earth, to give all who are parched from loss and destruction or burnt from the harsh realities of life, joy and beauty and purpose.

Our once subjugated lands must be taught to speak; to tell their stories, to give a voice to their oppression and longing for release into fulness of being and of life, where once they were taught to express themselves in the hostile and intolerant language of empire. The Protestant missionary activity that became prevalent during the colonial period reflected this tone in its proclamation of the gospel. No longer was it a gospel that freed an individual to be what God wanted one to be, but freedom was to acquire this British / European way of being at the death of one's inherent self. No doubt it would be said that it was a death to demon influences and a rising to a new, higher, and more civilised life. In this regard the church lost the ability to convey the saving grace of God and breathed the proud language of empire, but the gospel would not lose such grace intrinsic to its very nature, for by its own self it is 'the power of God unto salvation to everyone who believes'. Rom. 1: 16.

The Caribbean Church attempts to attain such a level of moral holiness and sanitised being based on past and current influences so much that there is a refusal to have any sort of engagement or encounter with the 'undesirables' out of a blinkered attempt to preserve one's holiness. It runs counter to Jesus' command to roll away the stone (Jn. 11: 39), even though the folk around are up in arms because there would be a stench and a rotten body would taint their holiness and make them ritually unclean. We refuse to see, we bury our heads in the sand, and just will not contend with certain pressing and sensitive issues because that is not what being 'holy' is all about. Jesus' ministry was one of engagement with the undesirables of society, the outcasts, and the jamettised culture; with its prostitutes, publicans, lepers, and beggars, portraying the fallenness of the human condition in plain view. It is a humanity unredeemed spiritually, morally, and economically, in the fullest sense of the word as the Jamettised society did not have a place in the 'oikoumene', or the inhabited space. But if the church refuses to see then it lives in a false reality which segregates God's people into those who are good to keep and those good only to throw away. It is a false reality where sin and struggle with sinful institutions are non-existent. It is a deist approach that sees in God a means of merely transferring the burden of the world's problems and thus humanly avoiding them.

People desire to become whole and to be valued according to their intrinsic human dignity. The Cartesian formula of Rene Descartes, 'Cogito ergo sum', 'I think, therefore, I am,' becomes in reality, 'Sum ergo cogito', 'I am, therefore I think', in this conflict between 'sum' and 'cogito' expressed in Jesus' great I AM statement of being the Resurrection and the Life vs. 25. In the desire to become and not just to be, it is the person, because of who one is that one desires to become. The person is already possessed of innate desires and yearnings that are given expression in word and action. One can only conceive of what one is already possessed of and therefore is a subject with a self to acquire and not an object to be known. A person, therefore, creates oneself from faithful awareness of one's heritage, environment, and of all one's desires and urges and cultivation of one's inner potentialities which are then projected outwards. There is a dynamic relationship between the death and resurrection of Christ that brings forth new life and the creative forces of both nature and humanity, in a new and redeemed created order which he is bringing to birth in this sign.

The revelation of Jesus' glory through this sign vs. 40, climaxes with his chiefest revelation as the Son of God in his own glory and glorification through death and resurrection. Remember, this glory refers not so much to *'shekinah'* or splendour and majesty, as to *'chabod'*, or the presence of God among his people, "...but I have said this for the sake of the crowd standing here, so that they may believe that you sent me." vs. 42b. In his resurrection he also reveals humankind's true estate which they are destined to regain in him, the Resurrection and the Life, vs. 25; the original image and likeness of God in which they were created but which has become tarnished by sin. This is the ultimate call to become all that God originally intended for humankind, which they can only gain through struggle, pain, and growth from imperfection to perfection. In a similar vein, Trinidad and Tobago Carnival is also a call to become a more just and equitable society by unmasking the realities behind the masks. There is a common link between the revelation of the *'chabod'*, glory or presence of God in Christ in the liturgical season leading to the climax of Carnival and the festival of Carnival itself in the God who struggles with his people, who knows, understands, and identifies with their longings, hopes, desires and frustrations, a God who lived in such a situation in Palestine. It is seen in a God who changes water into wine and thereby has power to transform the ordinary into the glorious. It is a God who engages actively with his people, the undesirables of society, neither scorning nor rejecting anything or anyone he has made, even though it "stinketh"; who even had a terrorist, Simon the Zealot, for a disciple, for that is what Zealots were to the Romans in that time. And out of this engagement God is able to bring healing and transformation to the twisted and distorted lives of the Jamettised society. "The dead man came out, his hands and feet bound with strips of cloth, and his face wrapped in a cloth. Jesus said to them, 'Unbind him, and let him go.' " vs. 44.

This task falls to the work of encoding and expressing the shape of the land in art, music, drama, and literature. It is the power of the Word made flesh, incarnate and dwelling among this people as part of its own; resembling, reflecting and redeeming its nature. Words are thoughts incarnate and therefore give an intelligible voice to one's deepest longings and desires. But it also calls them into being, as at the world's creation. The power of life and death are in the tongue. The breath of the mothering Spirit waits to give birth to all this Creative Word will say; hovering, brooding, incubating; this word is the land's spirit and its life. It is the lamp and light to the path to bene esse - giving direction for the shaping of a newly emerging society; creating it, calling forth its life, and giving guidance and validity; bringing order out of discord, weaving into one its many-rootedness. It is by the breath of the Spirit uttered by the Word made Flesh that the people enter into a new era of 'Pentecostal' engagement where each adapts to a common understanding of selfhood according to one's own intrinsic being, without stifling the 'otherness of others', even where that sense of being is drawn from many origins to form a new, more original, and locally adapted acknowledgement, understanding, and appreciation of a sense of nationhood.

GLOSSARY: Jamettised society – a term derived from the French word Diametre and phonetically pronounced in Trinidad and Tobago as Jamette. It refers to the diameter of a circle and seeing that prostitutes were usually very buxom women, having as it were, large 'diameters' they were referred to as Jamettes. Furthermore, since these women and other such ill-reputed persons came from the lower strata of society, they were said to fall 'below the diameter of respectable society', and thus became known as the Jamettised class.

NOTE:
1. Commentary on Genesis by Arthur S. Peake, Peake's Commentary on the Bible, Ed. A. S. Peake, Thos. Nelson and Sons Ltd. 1919, pg. 156.

EPILOGUE

The idea of the 'Word' becoming flesh and dwelling among humankind was restricted solely to the unique human person of Jesus Christ, and his limited human existence at one place and time in human history in Palestine. God's redemption of humankind in Jesus Christ is not limited to people, nor is it completed in it. It is a continuing process that involves the whole created order or cosmos; the physical/material, the moral/ethical, cultural, political, social, economic, and religious; in other words a total interconnectedness of all states of being and doing. Life is a search for wholeness. People desire to be fully human, with disease and disappointment as well as strength and accomplishment, and be thus fully present with God and presented to God, who himself is fully present with his creation in Christ Jesus and who alone can make perfect the offering. The Word of God made flesh and dwelling among us as one of us calls into being a new and redeemed creation through an eschatological community of God's people made manifest in Christ; and in God's new world made possible through the death and resurrection of Christ.

Our Caribbean lands must be taught to speak; to tell their stories, to give a voice to their oppression and longing for release into fulness of being and of life. The Babel of tongues and peoples must enter into a new Pentecost, where each feels one's sense of being in one's intrinsic racial and cultural identity; and even where that sense of being is drawn from many origins and ancestral ties to form a new, more original and locally adapted acknowledgement, understanding, and appreciation of being firmly rooted in and belonging to this new landscape.

This task falls to the work of encoding and expressing the shape of the land in art, music, drama and literature. It is the power of the Word made flesh, incarnate and dwelling among this people as part of its own; resembling, reflecting and redeeming its nature. Words are thoughts incarnate and therefore give and intelligible voice to one's deepest longings and desires.

But it also calls them into being, as at the world's creation. The power of life and death are in the tongue. The breath of the native spirit waits to give birth to all this word will say; hovering, brooding, incubating; this word is the land's spirit and its life. It is the lamp and light to the path to bene esse - giving direction for the shaping of a newly emerging society; creating it, giving life and guidance and validity; bringing order out of discord, weaving into one its many-rootedness.

The poet Elizabeth Browning acutely observes,
"Earth's crammed with heaven,
And every common bush afire with God..." (1).
The glory or manifest presence of God can be found in nature, in Word and Sacrament, through the action of God's eschatological community who, by the presence and power of the Holy Spirit, continue and extend the incarnation of Jesus Christ in time and space as his mystical Body on earth. Earth is crammed with heaven. It is full, chock-full of divine activity that leads it on to the perfect day.

The intrinsic grace of the Christian gospel can be described as having prophetic voice and pilgrim quality. Prophetic, because the gospel must be rooted in the particular geographical and historical experience of the people; Emmanuel, God with us; and must call into being the new humanity, the eschatological community of God's people made manifest in Christ; and in God's new world made possible through the death and resurrection of Christ. Pilgrim, because the gospel must always witness to the faith journey of the people and the accompanying new creation of the foregoing prophetic counter-culture. The prophetic grace of the gospel critiques and baptises the culture and local landscape, thus bringing it into the new and redeemed order of creation; through identification with the person and work of Christ.

"But only [he] who sees, takes off [his] shoes,
The rest sit round it and pluck blackberries,
And daub their faces unaware
More and more from the first similitude." (2)

This goal is attained by faith, by the pure in heart who shall see God because their intentions and purposes are sincere and who seek to follow by faith in closest communion and fellowship with the Divine.
Let there arise a people of prophetic grace and pilgrim quality!
"In the wasteland may Glory shine; in the land of the lost may the King make his home!" (3)

NOTES:
1. Elizabeth Browning 1806-1861, Earth's Crammed with Heaven.
2. ibid.
3. Ray Simpson, Celtic Worship Through the Year pg. 17; Hodder and Stoughton, London UK (c) 1997.

www.ingramcontent.com/pod-product-compliance
Lightning Source LLC
LaVergne TN
LVHW041555070526
838199LV00046B/1970